The Strange
Pawprint

Written by **SALLY GRINDLEY**
Illustrated by **JO BROWN**

ORCHARD BOOKS

Constable Tiggs

Sergeant Bumble

Albert

One cold, snowy morning, the
Bear Detectives were woken by
a loud knocking.
"Wake up! Wake up!" somebody
shouted.

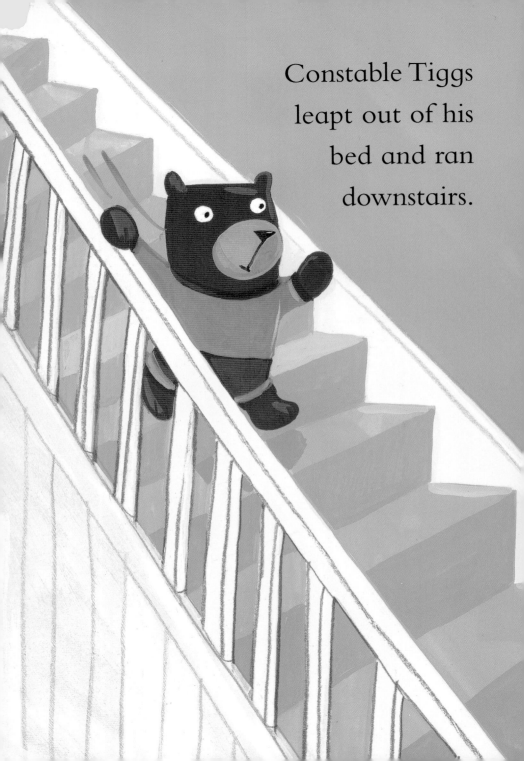

Constable Tiggs
leapt out of his
bed and ran
downstairs.

He found Albert, the repair-bear,
on the doorstep. "What on earth
has happened?" he said, shivering.

"I was checking the ground for holes, which is difficult in all this snow, when I found a strange pawprint," said Albert.

"What sort of strange?" asked Tiggs. "It looks as if the thing that made it has no fur, no pads and no hooves," said Albert. "And there are more strange pawprints in the park."

"I'd better fetch Sergeant Bumble," said Tiggs.

He bounded upstairs and knocked on his bedroom door. "Wake up, Sergeant Bumble!" he called.

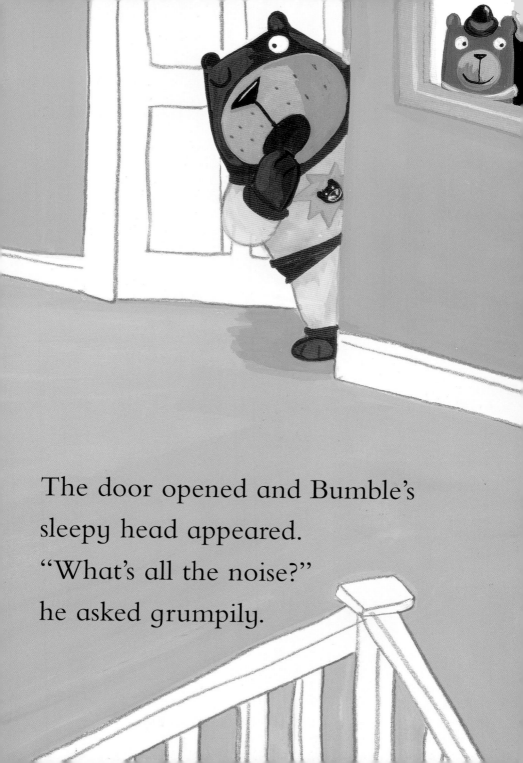

The door opened and Bumble's
sleepy head appeared.
"What's all the noise?"
he asked grumpily.

"Albert's found a strange pawprint in the snow. The thing that made it has no fur and no pads and no hooves," said Tiggs.

"Then we must have a look at it,"
said Bumble. "Get dressed, Constable
Tiggs, quickly now!"

A few minutes later, the two
detectives followed Albert to
the first pawprint.

"You're right, Albert," Bumble nodded, studying it closely. "That is very strange."

"What do you think made it?"
asked Albert.

"Something very large," said Bumble. "This is serious! We must tell everyone to stay indoors until we find out who, or what, made this pawprint."

They set off through the snow,
knocking on doors and warning
the villagers to stay inside.

When at last they had spoken to all of them, they headed back to the police house to search through their Book of Unusual Pawprints.

"Now, let me see," said Bumble.

"Could it be a turtle?"

"No, Sir," said Tiggs. "Turtles have
flippers and pointy toes."

"A penguin, perhaps?" asked Bumble.

"Too small," said Tiggs.

"What about an elephant, then?" asked Bumble.

"It could be an elephant!" cried Tiggs excitedly. "They're very big and they haven't got fur or pads or hooves."

"We'll have to go outside and
see if we can spot the scoundrel,"
said Bumble.

It was snowing harder. Every little
sound made them jump.

"I'm s-scared," shivered Tiggs.

"No need to be scared, Constable
Tiggs. It's my duty to protect my
officers as well as the village."
When they reached the place
outside the park where the
pawprint had been, it wasn't
there any more.

"It's gone!" exclaimed Bumble.
"The snow must have filled it in,"
explained Tiggs.
"Of course," said Bumble quickly.
"That's just what I was going to say."

The other pawprints
had gone as well. Tiggs
began to shiver as they
searched to see if any
new ones had appeared.

"I think we'd better go back into the warm," said Bumble. "If that elephant has any sense it won't come out again today."

They hurried back to the police house, where they sat in front of the fire and warmed their feet.

"It is hard being a detective sometimes," mused Bumble. "While we face great danger, the other villagers can feel safe behind closed doors."

"Do you think we'll find some
more pawprints in the
morning?" asked Tiggs.
"I won't be surprised if
we do," said Bumble.

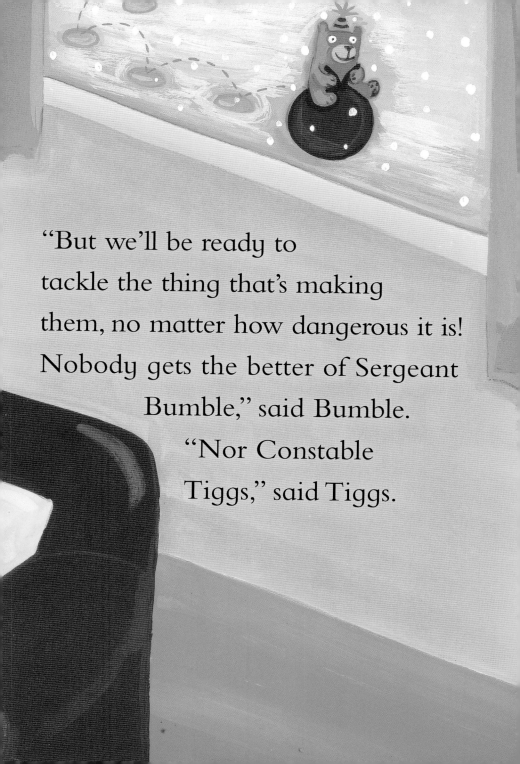

"But we'll be ready to
tackle the thing that's making
them, no matter how dangerous it is!
Nobody gets the better of Sergeant
Bumble," said Bumble.
"Nor Constable
Tiggs," said Tiggs.

THE BEAR DETECTIVES

SALLY GRINDLEY & JO BROWN

Bucket Rescue	978 1 84616 160 5
Who Shouted Boo?	978 1 84616 159 9
The Ghost Train	978 1 84616 161 2
Treasure Hunt	978 1 84616 158 2
The Mysterious Earth	978 1 84616 163 6
The Strange Pawprint	978 1 84616 164 3
The Missing Spaghetti	978 1 84616 165 0
A Very Important Day	978 1 84616 162 9

All priced at £4.99

Orchard Colour Crunchies are available from all good bookshops,
or can be ordered direct from the publisher:
Orchard Books, PO BOX 29, Douglas IM99 1BQ
Credit card orders please telephone 01624 836000
or fax 01624 837033 or visit our website: www.orchardbooks.co.uk
or e-mail: bookshop@enterprise.net for details.

To order please quote title, author and ISBN
and your full name and address.
Cheques and postal orders should be made payable to 'Bookpost plc.'
Postage and packing is FREE within the UK
(overseas customers should add £2.00 per book).

Prices and availability are subject to change.